Story play™

This book belongs to

_____ .

This book was read by

_____

on

_____ .

Are you ready to start reading the **StoryPlay** way?

Read the story on its own. Play the activities together
as you read!

Ready. Set. Smart!

To Barbie, Debbie, and Michele — K.G.
For Calvin and Elle — G.F.

Scholastic Inc., 557 Broadway, New York, NY 10012
Scholastic UK Ltd., Euston House, 24 Eversholt Street, London NW1 1DB

We're Going on a Spooky Ghost Hunt

by Ken Geist

illustrated by Guy Francis

CARTWHEEL BOOKS • AN IMPRINT OF SCHOLASTIC INC.

We're going on a spooky ghost hunt.
We're going to catch a ghost.
It's a dark and scary night.

We are not afraid!

BUMP!

BUMP!

We're coming to a hill.
A stumpy, bumpy hill.
Can't go around it. Can't go over it.
We have to march down it!

TWIST

We're coming to a path.
A misty, twisty path.
Can't go around it. Can't go over it.
We have to follow it!

Can you name some of the animals inside the forest?

TWIST

TWIST

We are not afraid.

We're coming to a bridge.
A wiggly, wobbly bridge.
Can't go around it. Can't go over it.
We have to walk on it!

We're going on a spooky ghost hunt.
We're going to catch a ghost.
It's a dark and scary night.

We are not afraid!

Would YOU be afraid?
Why or why not?

We're coming to a gate.
A squeaky, creaky gate.
Can't go around it. Can't go over it.
We have to go through it!

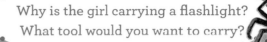

Why is the girl carrying a flashlight?
What tool would you want to carry?

SQUEAK

We are not afraid.

We're coming to some stairs.
Some steepy, creepy stairs.
Can't go around them. Can't go over them.
We have to climb up them!

We are not afraid.

We're coming to a door.
A scary, hairy door.
Can't go around it. Can't go over it.
We have to open it!

Can you find the hidden spider?

Ghosts Go Here

We are not afraid.

Does the ghost have enough drinks for everyone?

Oh no, it's a spooky ghost!

Fast!
Open the scary,
hairy door.

Down the
steepy,
creepy
stairs.

Through the squeaky,
creaky gate.

Across the wiggly, wobbly bridge.

Follow the misty, twisty path.

Up the stumpy, bumpy hill.

Inside the house.
Turn on the lights.
Run upstairs.

Uh-oh!
Forgot to shut
the door!

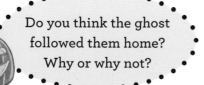

Do you think the ghost
followed them home?
Why or why not?

Jump into bed.
Pull up the covers.
WE'RE NEVER GOING ON A
SPOOKY GHOST HUNT AGAIN!!

Story time fun never ends with these creative activities!

★Ready, Set, Action!★

Do you remember all of the sounds the kids acted out during their adventure? Now it's your turn to act them out, too! Make sure to say the sounds while you act them out. Ready?

- Bump, bump, bump down the hill
- Twist, twist, twist along the path
- Wobble, wobble, wobble across the bridge
- Squeak, squeak, squeak through the gate
- Creep, creep, creep up the stairs

Now make up some sounds of your own to act out!

★ Ghost Story Time ★

Did you notice that the ghost appears on the very first page of the story? Great! The ghost seems to be following the kids, and when they finally see him inside the haunted house, he's doing something unexpected. Now's your chance to tell your own story about the ghost! Go back through the book and pay attention to what he's doing on every page. Then use that information to help craft your story. Happy storytelling!